Looking at ROCKS

By Jennifer Dussling

Illustrated by
Deborah and Allan Drew-Brook-Cormack
and Tim Haggerty

Grosset & Dunlap • New York

Rocks Are Everywhere!

Rocks are in the ocean,
underground, on the beach,
and in the mountains.
Some buildings are made of rocks.
Some roads are, too.

Looking at ROCKS

Library of Congress Cataloging-Publication Data is available.

photo credits: cover © Charles D. Winters/Photo Researchers, Inc.; p. 10 © Dennis Flaherty/Photo Researchers, Inc.; p. 11 © Hervé Berthoule/Jacana/Photo Researchers, Inc.; p. 12 © E. R. Degginger/Photo Researchers, Inc.; p. 14 © Joyce Photographics/Photo Researchers, Inc.; p. 16 © Charles D. Winters/Photo Researchers, Inc.; p. 18 © A.W. Ambler/Photo Researchers, Inc.; p. 20 © Gary Retherford/Photo Researchers, Inc.; p. 21 © Reggie David Productions/Pacific Stock; p. 24 © Biophoto Associates/Photo Researchers, Inc.; p. 26 © Joyce Photographics/Photo Researchers, Inc.; p. 28 © M. Claye/Jacana/Photo Researchers, Inc.; p. 30 © Andrew J. Martinez/Photo Researchers, Inc.; p. 32 © John R. Foster/Photo Researchers, Inc.; p. 34 © Charles D. Winters/Photo Researchers, Inc.; p. 36 © Mark A. Schneider/Photo Researchers, Inc.; p. 38 © H. Armstrong Roberts/Stock Market Photo; p. 40 © Phillip Hayson/Photo Researchers, Inc.; p. 42 © Joyce Photographics/Photo Researchers, Inc.; p. 44 © Joyce Photographics/ Photo Researchers, Inc.

ISBN 0-448-42516-5   A B C D E F G H I J

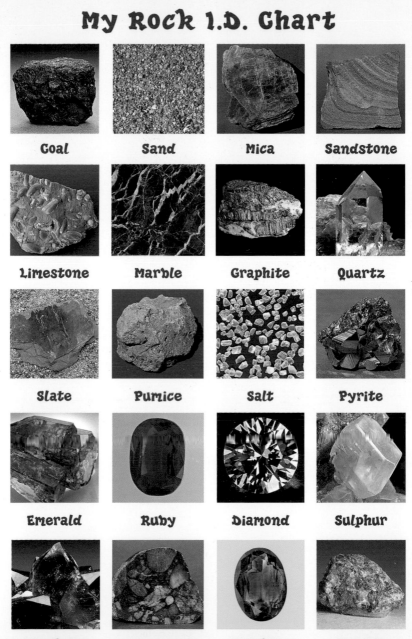

My Rock I.D. Chart

Coal	Sand	Mica	Sandstone
Limestone	Marble	Graphite	Quartz
Slate	Pumice	Salt	Pyrite
Emerald	Ruby	Diamond	Sulphur
Amethyst	Conglomerate	Sapphire	Granite

Our planet, Earth, is made mostly of rock
that is millions of years old.
The very center is metal.
Around it is a thick layer
of melted rock.
And the outer layer
of Earth is solid rock.

layers around center
(melted rock)

metal center

outer layer
(solid rock)

Want to be a Rock Hound?

People who collect rocks
are called "rock hounds."
You can be one, too!
Here is what you need:

___ long pants and a T-shirt (with long sleeves
    if you are in the woods)
___ boots or tough shoes
___ a hat if it's hot
___ water (just in case you get thirsty!)
___ a bag for your rocks
___ paper to wrap around the rocks
___ adhesive tape
___ scissors
___ a pencil
___ this book!

How to Use This Book

When you find a rock,
see if it is on your ID card.
Then find the pages in the book
about that rock.
Put your sticker on the page.

But maybe you can't tell what rock it is.
Just mark it with a number using
a little strip of tape.
Write the number on
the tape and
also write the number on a blank page
in the back of this book.

Your page can look like this:

Today's Date: August 7

Rock Number: 3

Type of rock: ???

It is: light brown

The rock is: Oval

It is: Small

I found it: In my yard

Notes: The rock is smooth and shiny. It is a little pointy on one side.

Maybe a teacher or other grown-up can tell you more about the rock.
It's easy to find rocks.
Just open your eyes and look around.
So turn the page to get started!

Quartz

One of the most common rocks is quartz.
(You say it: kwortz)
Quartz looks like glass.
But it is much harder.
It can scratch most other rocks.
It comes in lots of colors, like pink,
brown, yellow, green, blue . . .

close-up of quartz crystals

. . . and purple!
Purple-colored
quartz is called
amethyst.

I found
quartz

place your
sticker here

Sand

Most people look for
shells at the beach.
You can look for
rocks. It will not
be hard. Rocks
are everywhere
on the beach.
That's because
sand is made
of rocks! Over
time, the rocks
broke down
into tiny bits.
Almost every
grain of sand is
an itty-bitty piece
of quartz.

Try it!

Spread some sand
on white paper.
Look at it with a magnifying glass.
What colors do you see?

___black

___ clear

___ white

___pink

I found
sand

Sandstone

Sandstone is just what it sounds like. It is a stone made of sand. During dinosaur times, rivers washed sand into the sea. More sand settled on top. The bottom layers of sand became stone. Rocks made in layers like this are called sedimentary.

Try it!

It's easy to tell if you've found sandstone.
Rub it with your fingers.
Does it feel grainy?
Do bits of sand come off on your fingers?
It's sandstone!

The Grand Canyon is made of
sandstone and limestone.
You can see stripes in
the canyon walls.
Each stripe is one layer of rock.

I found
sandstone

place your
sticker here

Mica

Mica (you say it: MY-ka) is dark and silvery. It splits into very thin sheets. Mica has many layers. You can peel them apart.

Try it!

Try peeling off mica.

How thin you can get the layer?

Can you see through it?

Can you bend it without it breaking?

You may see mica in parking lot pavement.
If a shiny patch catches your eye,
take a closer look. It might be mica.

Granite

Did you find a speckled rock? It might be granite. (You say it: GRAN-ett)

Granite is a rock with lots of colors. Do you see gray and black and white and pink? Granite looks spotty because it is made up of different rocks. They all got pressed together.

On Mount Rushmore, the faces of
Presidents George Washington, Thomas
Jefferson, Theodore Roosevelt, and
Abraham Lincoln are carved from granite!

I found
granite

place your
sticker here

Sulphur

If you find sulphur
(you say it: SULL-fer),
you will know it.
Sulphur is bright
yellow! And it
smells a lot like
rotten eggs!

Sulphur is often found close to volcanoes.

I found
sulphur

place your
sticker here

Rock Recipe

Did you ever read a cereal box?
It sometimes says:
"With 8 vitamins and minerals."
There are traces of minerals
in some foods.
Sulphur is a mineral.
There is sulphur
in oats and coconuts!
But sulphur can also be called a rock!
So what is the difference
between rocks and minerals?

Rocks vs. Minerals

Think of rocks this way.
There are basic foods and mixed foods.
Some rocks are basic, like milk or eggs.
These rocks are called minerals.
Other rocks are mixed, like cake.
Cake is made of the milk and eggs.
Granite is like cake.
It is made of rocks like quartz and mica.

Rocks	Minerals
marble	diamond
limestone	halite
coal	mica
granite	quartz
sandstone	sulphur
pumice	graphite
conglomerate	pyrite
slate	

Limestone

Limestone is partly made of the shells of sea creatures. These creatures lived millions of years ago. Over time, their shells and bones stuck together. They became rock.

History rocks

Guess what famous buildings are made of limestone? If you said the pyramids, you are right. They are made of limestone blocks.

Look at limestone closely.
If you are lucky, you will
see little fossils.

I found
limestone

place your
sticker here

Marble

Marble is a pretty rock. Sometimes it is black or red. Sometimes it is pure white. Sometimes it has swirls of color.

All marble was once limestone.
Deep in the earth, the limestone was
squeezed very hard and became very hot.
Then it changed to marble.
Rocks that change like this
are called metamorphic.
(You say it: mett-ah-MORE-fick)

Many beautiful statues are carved from marble blocks. You'll also see a lot of marble in buildings like fancy hotels and banks.

I found
marble

place your
sticker here

Graphite

This gray rock is graphite. (You say it: GRAFF-ite) Graphite is soft. It also feels kind of greasy and smudges anything that it touches.

Rock your world

You see graphite every day. The gray core of your pencil is graphite.

These mine workers are looking for diamonds. The diamonds used to be graphite! That's because graphite can change.

If graphite is very deep in the earth and if it is squeezed very hard by rocks around it, it turns into a diamond!

I found
graphite

Slate

Slate is usually gray.
But sometimes it can be red
or green or black.
Still it's easy to spot.
When slate breaks,
it splits into smooth, flat sheets.

Rock your world

Slate is often used on roofs.
Chalkboards are made of slate.
Maybe you knew that.
But did you know you write on
chalkboards with another rock?
Chalk is a special kind of limestone!

Got Chalk?

I found
slate

place your
sticker here

Pumice

You may have some pumice in your bathroom. People sometimes use it to scrub away dry skin. Think you found a piece? Drop it in a bowl of water. Pumice is so light, it floats like a sponge—and it kind of looks like a sponge, too!

But pumice is not a sponge. It is cooled lava. Lava is the melted rock that shoots out of volcanoes. When the lava cools down, it becomes hard. The hardened lava is pumice!

All the little holes in pumice are bubbles that were in the hot lava. Rocks that are made from melted rock are called igneous.
(You say it: IG-nee-us)

I found
pumice

place your
sticker here

Salt

You can go rock collecting at the dinner table! Just pick up a couple grains of salt. Salt is a clear or white mineral. It has another fancy name, too—halite (you say it: HAY-ite). Take a close look at salt with a magnifying glass. Each grain is really a tiny cube.

Here, Mom, season your salad with some rocks!

Try it!

Next time you go to the beach,
bring back a jar of ocean water.
(Warning: Don't drink it!)

Pour the water into a shallow pan.

Put the pan in a sunny place.

The water will dry up.

But you will see
something left over.
That's salt!

I found
salt

(It's not good to taste it!)

Coal

Coal is a hard, shiny, black rock. But long, long ago, it was green. Coal is made from really old plants. Millions of years ago, ferns and plants and trees grew around a swamp.

water

silt and mud

compressed plants and trees

After they died,
they dropped into the water.
They did not rot away.
A thick layer of sand
covered the plants.
Over time, the heavy sand
pressed down on the plants.
They turned into coal.

sand

coal

I found
coal

place your
sticker here

workers delivering coal to a home

Thousands of years ago, people mostly burned wood in fires. Then someone found out that coal burns, too. It doesn't give off a lot of smoke like wood. But it does pollute the air. Today homes are heated by gas or electricity.

Is Charcoal Coal?

Charcoal isn't coal.
It isn't even a rock!
Charcoal is just burned wood.
So why don't people use wood
in their grills?
Sometimes wood is not all the way dry.
It also can have dirt and stuff in it.
Charcoal is always dry and clean.
And it lights easily!

Diamond

Diamonds are very rare rocks. But maybe someone you know has one. Diamonds are often used in jewelry.

The largest diamond ever found weighed over a pound!
Fake diamonds are called rhinestones.
They are not real rocks.
You will only find them in stores.

Rock Rainbow

Rare rocks like diamonds
are called gemstones.
Some popular gemstones
are emeralds, sapphires, rubies,
and amethysts. Do you know their colors?
Then put their stickers
in the box next to their names.

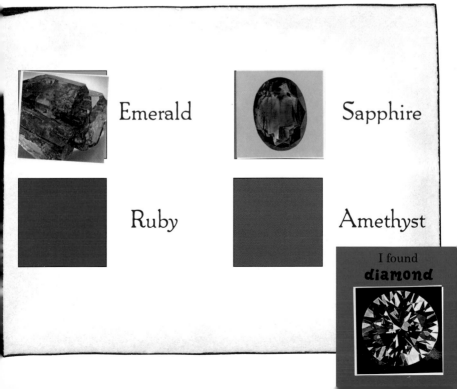

Emerald

Sapphire

Ruby

Amethyst

I found
diamond

Conglomerate

This is a funny looking rock.

It's called conglomerate (you say it: kon-GLAHM-eh-rett). It's made of all sorts of pebbles stuck together. Sometimes some of the pebbles are rare rocks. If you are really, really lucky, you may find a ruby there!

I found
conglomerate

place your
sticker here

Be a Rock Artist!

All you need are some paints, paintbrushes, and a smooth oval rock. Wash and dry the rock, then follow the steps. (Let each coat of paint dry before adding another color!)

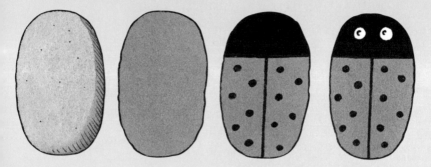

1. Start with your clean, dry rock.
2. Paint the whole rock with red paint.
3. Using the black paint, paint the head, a stripe down the middle, and spots.
4. Paint 2 eyes with white paint.

You've painted a ladybug!

This is just one idea to get you started. You will have the most fun making your own creations! If the rock is large, you can use it as a paperweight. Use smaller painted rocks to decorate your desk or windowsill.

Fool's Gold

Hooray! It's gold! Or, at least, it looks like gold. This rock is pyrite. (You say it: PIE-rite) It fools lots of people. That's why it's also called fool's gold.

How can you tell gold from fool's gold? Real gold is softer. You can dent real gold with your nail. You can't dent fool's gold!

Rock tricks

There are some tests to help
tell different rocks apart.
If you rub a rock across a tile,
it leaves a colored streak.
What color streak do you think pyrite makes?
Surprise! Pyrite makes a green-black streak.

I found
fool's gold

place your
sticker here

You found your rocks.
Now show them off!
Egg cartons are good
for small rocks.
You can put one rock
in each "cup."
Make a label for the rocks you know.

Then put them in order.
You can group them by size.
You can group them by color.
You can put all the smooth ones together
and all the rough ones together.

Best of all,
your collection can grow
bigger and bigger and bigger.
After all, rocks are all over!

Looking at ROCKS

My Field Notes

*Use these pages to write down or draw what you see when you are looking at rocks. Write the name of each rock and describe it.

*Don't forget: Describe the rock in your notes even if you can't tell from this book what kind it is. Maybe later you will see the rock in another book!

Today's date: _____

Rock number: _____

Name of rock: _____

Color: _____

Shape: _____

Size: _____

Where I found it: _____

My notes: _____
_____
_____
_____
_____

You can draw here!

Today's date: _____

Rock number: _____

Name of rock: _____

Color: _____

Shape: _____

Size: _____

Where I found it: _____

My notes: _____

_____

_____

_____

_____

You can draw here!

Today's date: _____

Rock number: _____

Name of rock: _____

Color: _____

Shape: _____

Size: _____

Where I found it: _____

My notes: _____

_____

_____

_____

_____

You can draw here!

Today's date: _____

Rock number: _____

Name of rock: _____

Color: _____

Shape: _____

Size: _____

Where I found it: _____

My notes: _____

_____

_____

_____

_____

You can draw here!

Today's date:

Rock number:

Name of rock:

Color:

Shape:

Size:

Where I found it:

My notes:

You can draw here!

Today's date: _____

Rock number: _____

Name of rock: _____

Color: _____

Shape: _____

Size: _____

Where I found it: _____

My notes: _____

_____

_____

_____

_____

You can draw here!

Today's date:

Rock number:

Name of rock:

Color:

Shape:

Size:

Where I found it:

My notes:

You can draw here!